HALLOWEEN MACHINE – KURTIS PRIMM

If you want some spooky fun
Pick up this magazine
Grab the newest issue of
The Halloween Machine

Interviews and pictures
It's got articles and poems
It covers scary subjects
And the haunts in peoples homes

Halloweens from years gone by
And all that's current too
It's in the Halloween Machine
And sure to interest you

So many things make Halloween
An awesome holiday
From ancient legends years ago
To stories told today

It's scary movies, scary books
And even monster songs
The imagery and spooky games
Come on and play along

From cardboard decorations
To new Hi-tech DVDs
We cover all things spooky
In the Halloween Machine

If you're looking for a smile
Or a trip down memory lane
It's right here on the pages
Of this awesome magazine

From cover through to cover
And the pages in between
All the spooky things you love
In the Halloween Machine!

Halloween Machine logo: Nate Barrett

ISBN: 978-1-300-14499-1

HALLOWEEN MACHINE

VOL. 1 Issue 3 **September 2012 $8**

CONTENTS

Too Old to Trick or Treat?!

By Paul Counelis

Every year around Halloween, this question inevitably comes up in different internet forums and social pages from all around the world: "How old is too old to 'Trick 'R Treat'?

People are VERY opinionated about the subject, unsurprisingly. It makes for a somewhat divided Halloween community, as well. Some say that it's only for kids; others say there's no age limit for Halloween fun. Still others think that it's ok to go out Trick or Treating on that magical night at virtually any age, as long as you're wearing a costume. I think I agree with the third opinion.

My mother goes out with her grandkids every year, and I watch the joy that the kids get out of her going up to the door with them. She dresses up in a "boogeyman" costume, which is also a source of amusement throughout the night. A few people here and there have complained about an adult going out with the kids, but most people think it's fun and a great way to create memories. A lot of smiles happen.

In terms of an exact age, I think it's nonsense, really. I love to see teenagers out, dressed in costume, running around having good clean fun. Halloween is for EVERYBODY…it's the perfect night to be a kid, or even to recapture, for a few hours, what it was like to be a kid. Because, after all, there really is no other night like Halloween throughout the year; people should celebrate it in whatever way brings them and those around them the most joy.

What do YOU think? 

SCREAMER Premieres!

Media Release

"Everybody's open....but us," haunt operator Phil Granger offers up in the film *Screamer*, which is getting ready to come out on VOD, DVD and having it's premiere in Jeffersonville, Indiana at a special event at the Sheraton Riverside Hotel.

Screamer, which follows the activities of a couple of struggling haunt owners in Indiana, has been in and out of production since 2005. In the latest back slide of development, the film went back into shooting again in February of 2012 to record yet another set-back for Granger and his partner Matt Kemp. The two are no strangers to adversity. Just barely able to survive a haunt season, in the film Kemp drives around in a car which has 250,000 miles on it and has two coffee cans for headlights. Despite having two other part time jobs, Kemp seems determined to pull off the season no matter what the cost.

"I have just a little over a month, yeah about a month and I have three months of stuff to do."

Screamer was originally conceived as a haunted attraction travelogue. Director William N. McHugh was inspired by the film *The Happy Haunting of America* that he checked out of local library. By the time the film had been in production for over two years, it was pretty obvious that *Screamer* was going to be a different film.

"We shot many haunts and also Iron Stock and Hauntcon for the film. I think many people in the industry were a little puzzled that the footage was nowhere to be found after a few years. But, you can't meet these guys (Granger/Kemp) and not be on their side, it's like they suck you in with their enthusiasm, so we decided to tell their story even though it took a lot longer."

While the documentary doesn't dig down deep into the lives of Granger, Kemp and their friend Jamie Taylor, it does go deep enough to reveal some of the pitfalls of haunted house ownership and without the guidance or setup of a reality TV show.

"All we did was set up a camera, place microphones and record. If they argued or something went wrong we recorded it, but we never manufactured anything here."

And indeed, things do go wrong. The haunt located in New Albany is shut down by the local fire marshal before it can even open, actors and crew blow up over missing pay, short preparation time shows up in the poor performances by actors and Kemp reflects on poor business decisions that are wreaking havoc on his personal passion.

"Someone decided that everyone would be willing to pay five dollars and everyone has five dollars in their pocket, so here we stand and it makes us look like we're not worth as much."

Kemp's lament seems to be echoed by legendary haunt consultant Leonard Pickel, who also appears in the film to warn people about the dangers of being swept up by the haunted attraction business.

"People go around haunted attractions, count heads the weekend before Halloween and think, 'Wow, this guy's making a bundle'. If it was that easy, everyone would be doing it."

Screamer Director McHugh says he has seen this same mentality first hand.

"Someone walked out of a haunt, did some fuzzy math and complained loudly that Granger and Kemp must be pulling in $18,000 a night on the haunt. It's the most ridiculous thing I have ever heard. A lot of these people including Matt and Phil barely survive; they do it because they love putting on a show."

Some successful haunts are featured in the film such as The Baxter Avenue Morgue, The Haunted Hotel, Dead Acres, Nightmare on 13th and Necropolis City of Perpetual Darkness. However, in an interview, Larry Kirchner, owner of The Darkness, warns Halloween lovers how even successful haunted houses can affect your outlook on the holiday.

"You're really busy all summer. I have always loved Halloween but because this is a business, it doesn't mean as much to me as it used to."

The director, who also became involved with haunted houses after starting the film, says his experience in the haunt industry has come full circle.

"I met Matt and Phil seven years ago when I started the film. I've learned everything I wanted to know about the haunted house business and perhaps some things I didn't want to know....after I documented a final catastrophic loss, it was finally time to release the film."

Screamer won an award at the Las Vegas Film Festival earlier this year but McHugh didn't attend the event in order to premiere the film in the Kentucky and Indiana area where it was shot.

"The film was shot here, it made sense to premiere it here with others in the local haunted house business involved."

For more information & tickets for the Screamer Film Premiere, go to ScreamerEvent.com.

LET THEM COME – Kurtis Primm

I've been workin hard all year
With not one day of rest
Hours spent, up late all night
To make my work the best

And now October has arrived
And all my work is done
And I've got just one thing to say
And I say "Let them come"

I'll give them what they want to see
What they've come to expect
A Halloween extravaganza
Built with toil and sweat

The zombie stands at ready
And the ghost is in the crypt
The speakers wait to spring to life
Once the switch is flipped

All year I work for Halloween
Until my hands are numb
Tonight's the night we've waited for
And I say "Let them come"

The witch stands silent in the yard
And waits to stir her pot
Her glassy eye falls square on me
And waits for me to nod

The darkness falls and down the street
I hear the growing hum
As people start to gather
And I say "Let them come"

I see them drawing closer
And it's time to flip the switch
The ghosts cry out together
In a haunting perfect pitch

Barricade the doors.

Board up the windows.

Try to survive the NIGHT.

A MATT CLOUDE FILM

NIGHT OF THE LIVING DEAD GENESIS

VIRGO SQUARED PICTURES PRESENTS A MATT CLOUDE FILM
NIGHT OF THE LIVING DEAD: GENESIS SARAH SNYDER MIKE LORD Sr. DAVID WITT
DONNA GEE ROUSSEAU CYRUS SAMSON CHRISTY JOHNSON JIM KRUT DAVID CRAWFORD
HEIDI HINZMAN WITH BRENLEIGH RIGSBEE AND JUDITH O'DEA AS BARBRA
LEAD PRODUCTION ASSISTANT KATIE BENNETT PRODUCTION ASSISTANTS EDWIN KOESTER AND WAYLON K. SMITH
MUSIC BY WAYLON K. SMITH AND RACHEL VAUGHN DIRECTOR OF PHOTOGRAPHY ROBERT W. FILION
EXECUTIVE PRODUCER CARLO ALVAREZ CO-WRITTER WIL SMITH CO-WRITTEN/ PRODUCED AND DIRECTED BY MATT CLOUDE

http://www.facebook.com/NOTLD2012

They're coming to get you again...SOON

THIS FILM IS NOT YET RATED

SPOTLIGHT – MAKEUP ARTIST /EFX ARTIST

LAURA DENOTARIS

Laura DeNotaris is a makeup artist based out of Morris County, NJ. Growing up, she was frightened—yet fascinated—by the horror movies her parents didn't want her watching. Halloween serves as her favorite holiday, and over the years, Laura transformed herself into ingenious characters, celebrity look-alikes and everything in between. It wasn't until 2010, while decked out and parading at a Zombiewalk that she sought to take her love of makeup a step further. The horror film enthusiast and aspiring makeup artist then decided to marry her two passions together and pursue it as a career. Upon completion of extensive and intricate makeup schooling, internships and certifications, Laura is now making her unique mark on the world as a special effects makeup artist. To learn more about Laura and view her work, visit: LDeNotaris.com.

3RD Degree Forehead – Laura DeNotaris

These burns were created by applying 3rd Degree, a product mixture of two different types of silicone. I applied it irregularly to parts of the skin, and then picked at select blisters to create a "popped" effect. In order to do this, I sunk holes in the centers of the blisters with tweezers before the silicone was completely dry. Once dried, I applied several layers of liquid latex over the entire area.

Now, the fun begins: I carefully ran closed tweezers along the latex on the skin to pick pieces up, and allowed them to fold back into other areas of skin. This produces the appearance that the flesh has not only opened up, but has melted and adhered to various other parts of the general area.

I then stippled red RMG paint over the entire affected area to create irritation. Next, I painted the outsides of the blisters (as well as some of the insides of the opened ones) in a bruise-like color to create depth and shadow. For finishing touches, I lightly brushed a black cream color over the highpoints to show charring. At this point, it was easy to see which of the blisters look nastiest, so I took it a step further by mixing a mustard color with some castor oil, and added it to the insides of the blisters to show apparent, oozing infected pus.

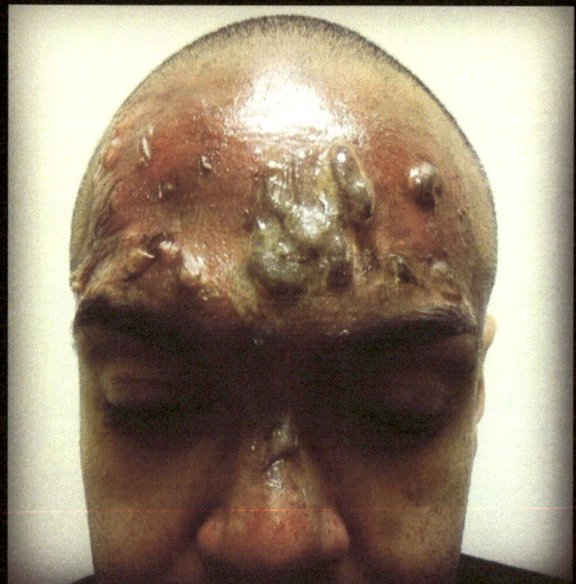

Melting Wicked Witch – Laura DeNotaris

When I found this great 4-piece foam latex facial prosthetic that appears it is in the process of melting, I was immediately inspired to create my own rendition of the Wicked Witch.

I first did a test-fit of the pieces on my model to ensure proper placement. This is always a helpful step to save you the trouble of accidentally gluing on crooked pieces. The foam latex prosthetics were applied with an adhering agent called Pros-aide. Next, I filled in the edges of where the prosthetic meets the skin with a filling agent called Bondo. I applied as many layers as it needed until there weren't any edges left—they need to appear seamless. This is the most important step of the application because if your final work shows the edges, it will not sell the character or illusion you are trying to create.

Once I was happy with my edges, or lack thereof, I started my paint job. I used green and yellow RMG paints, making sure the green was darkest in the shadow areas and beginning of the drips. The middle of the drip was painted in a green-yellow to show the transition on pigment melting away, and finally, the tips of the drips were painted in a pale yellow, along with some castor oil to give it an extra shine.

Alcohol paint colors in dark and light browns, as well as yellow, were then spattered all over, which helped to break up the opaqueness of the green, as well as provide some life-like texture to the prosthetic. I was also mindful to muddy up my model's hands and arms. I applied the same green used in the face, along with some brown and purple cream colors and mottled it into the skin to create a blotchy, uneven appearance to show lowered blood flow to the surface of the skin.

The finishing touches are always what really make the character come to life. I smeared Ampro gel all over my model's face, hands and arms to illustrate that grime and wickedness seeping out of her pores. I also used Depp gel to saturate my model's hair entirely, and give it that extra stringy appearance. As for her rotting teeth, they were also mottled in Ben Nye's Tooth Color in nicotine, decay and black.

Last, but not least, I decided to incorporate a prop. I requested my model stand in the center of a hole in foam board that I had spray-painted in a stone-like texture. This was fastened around her waist to create the illusion she was melting into the concrete ground. Shooting her from an aerial view helped achieve the melting effect.

I thank everyone involved for their hard work and making my concept come to life!

Makeup Artist: Laura DeNotaris

Model: Linda DeNotaris

Photographer: Last Witness

Assistant: Elise Cortese

HALLOWEEN STORE SIGHTINGS

WITH AUDRIANA COUNELIS

This month our resident Halloween store expert Audriana Counelis, fresh off of her 11th birthday, pays a visit to perennial Halloween favorite 'Michael's'.

In mid-August I went to Michael's trying to find Halloween merchandise.

My parents and I walked in, and the smell.... MMMMM! Just like cinnamon and pumpkin spice mixed together. I saw fall leaves for crafts hanging everywhere. I ran to where the Halloween stuff usually is and it was like I dreaming! Halloween everywhere (that is like Heaven to me)!

There were awesome Lemax / Spooky Town knick knacks together on

Display as a huge Halloween village called Spooky Town. A really cool

building was the Broom Showroom. It has a window that in the inside you could see witches flying in circles on broomsticks. There was also an ice cream shop and truck that said "Frosty's Ice Scream" and a really awesome Candy Shop with all kinds of weird candied bugs.

They had pumpkins; plastic pumpkins that you could carve and they had all kinds of paint and stuff that people could decorate them with. I really like this

creepy crown pumpkin that someone had hand painted.

We walked down an aisle to find a black Halloween collar for cats, because we had just gotten a new orange cat (who we named Spookley). So I begged my dad to buy it for him and we did.

They had weird owls made out of like colored straw, black and orange. I love Halloween owls.

Also there was an orange mask and my dad said it made me look like an owl. There was also a witch mask it was wooden and it was made so someone could color it with markers. There were also tons of other really spooky and cool crafts and Halloween decorations.

Michael's is one of my favorites so go check it out for yourself. Next month JoAnn's…see you then!

Audri's parents got her the Lemax Candy Store for her birthday. Her birthday party is one day after this issue goes to press…shh, don't tell her.

Best Halloween Television Episodes

By Paul Counelis

Every October, when the air outside whispers a chill and the leaves start to fade with gold and red hues, the Halloween enthusiast starts to look forward to all the joys of autumn and the Halloween season.

Of course, taking long walks, playing in the leaves, looking at merchants' holiday related items and consuming apple cider and donuts are staples of the season, and what better way to set the mood for those activities than television Halloween episodes?

There are so many beloved Halloween shows that it would be beyond ridiculous to even attempt a "Top 10" list. The reasons why they're beloved are many, from the charm of the old *Happy Days* shows to the weird factor of *The Simpsons*, and with the sheer volume of episodes that are added to the canon each year, it's extremely subjective.

Here are just a few of our favorites at the Halloween Machine.

Two Guys, a Girl, and a Pizza Place: "Psycho Halloween". Even though this was a short lived series, the Halloween episode is memorable and fun, even a bit spooky. The gang winds up locked inside the pizza parlor, trying to decide between two versions of their friend Berg, the evil one and the good one. BONUS: Ryan Reynolds in an early role.

Roseanne: "Boo". No list of Halloween episodes would be complete without Roseanne and Dan Conner. Along with *Home Improvement*, Roseanne made Halloween a bit more fun every year with their creative surprises and laugh out loud antics. "Boo" might not be the absolute BEST of the Roseanne episodes, but it's the one that kicked off all of the Halloween shenanigans and entered it into television lore. And it IS pretty darn good.

The Cosby Show: "Halloween". This one falls squarely into the "charming" category, as the ever cool and wise Dr. and Mrs. Huxtable throw a Halloween party at their house, and Vanessa freaks out over the presence of "the coolest boy in the seventh grade". It's kind of strange that Cos and company never made more Halloween themed shows, because this one is so…well…charming.

Community: Every Halloween Episode. That might be a cop-out, but there's just no choosing between *Community*'s outstanding All Hallows tributes. From zombies to nerd frenzy, *Community* takes the rules and completely breaks them, playing with the conventions of both the sitcom and horror genres with equal success. Plus, they are flat out hilarious!

Disney Channel: "Halloween in April", "Monstober", etc. This might not be a popular choice among the older crowd, but there's no denying the fun that Disney Channel brings with their month long celebrations and various Halloween shows. Some of the best episodes of their genial but generally lukewarm offerings come from the magic of Halloween night. *Suite Life of Zack and Cody* has a

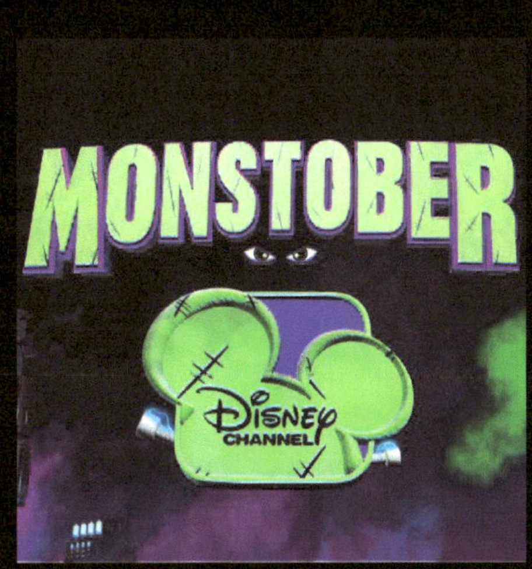

particularly amusing episode called "Arwinstein" that should appeal to Halloween addicts of any age. BONUS: Disney runs Halloween related movies every night in October.

Friends: "The One With the Halloween Party". Even though *Friends* ran for ten extremely successful seasons and has a throng of fans who hold the show near and dear, there are a number of detractors and critics of the show. Those naysayers notwithstanding, you'd have to hate the show pretty hardcore to not at least get a smile when Ross is forced to explain his costume because of it's uncanny resemblance to, er, walking feces.

Modern Family: "Halloween". One of TV's all time best sitcoms features one of the best Halloween episodes of all time. Do the math. Claire and Phil Dunphy (arguably one of the greatest TV characters ever) turn their house into a giant haunted house. However, this one doesn't run as smoothly as our friends the Conners' haunts used to…hilarity ensues. The yard décor and interior of the house are actually very creepy cool, with Phil scaring himself multiple times by his own well placed and effective animatronic.

SO, whaddya think? Which Halloween related episodes are the ones you look forward to watching every fall season? With the number of great ones out there and the new ones that are sure to pepper our television screens every year, there are so many to choose from.

I'm one of those Halloween fiends who will watch ANY Halloween episode from any series. Last week I watched early airings of Halloween shows from *Reba*, *What I Like About You* and yes, even *Beverly Hills 90210*.

For those of you wondering, the 90210 episode is really kinda fun. And having to admit that, my friends, is the peak of Halloween dorkdom.

THE TALE OF UNCLE JONAH

Charles Shaver

Uncle Jonah was a traveling preacher. Actually, he was a trucker, but he was also a Southern Baptist minister with the Glory to God Cornerstone Bible Church about thirty miles south of Flint, Michigan. He drove truck to pay the bills and feed eight children, he preached to pay off other debts.

He really was my uncle, but he had everyone call him Uncle Jonah, family or not.

Uncle Jonah was driving one night through the Ozarks. A single highway split a sea of pines so tall he couldn't see the Hunter's Moon making the sky glow gold. The darkness of the treeline enveloped his truck. Traffic was thin on the highway so late at night.

On the seat next to him sat a boom box. He'd found a local station replaying parts of the Newport Festival and Bob Dylan was screeching away over the little speakers. Uncle Jonah smiled and tapped the palms of his hands on the steering wheel in beat with the tune.

Quickly approaching in the road ahead of him was an enormous curve. Beyond the silhouetted trees the sky shifted from gold to indigo to bright yellow and back. The colors were thick and moved with sticky calmness. Uncle Jonah watched the living sky for a moment before he turned his attention back to the road, back to the approaching curve.

His hands stopped tapping.

He turned the wheel as the highway snaked around a stand of trees. He turned right as the highway slithered back. Coming around that second curve, his whole world lit up. Four cars had piled up in a burning mass on the highway ahead of him.

Uncle Jonah hit the brakes.

Bob Dylan slide off the seat. His electric life died.

Uncle Jonah jumped from the cab and ran for the fiery mess. Of the four cars there were eight people, all dead except two. A mother and daughter trapped in a Buick; the mother screaming for dear life, the daughter screaming and crying at her mother. The mother was pinned in place, a steering wheel pressing her chest. The daughter also pinned in place, the horror of her mother's screams immobilizing her.

Uncle Jonah ran to the passenger side of the car. Opening the door, he unfastened the daughter's seatbelt and ran with her to the tree line. She screamed in his ear the whole way, cries for mommy.

“Stay here,” he said as he set her down. “Do you hear me? Everything will be okay. Mommy will be okay. I’ll go get her now. Will you stay here?”

The daughter stopped her screaming, but not her sobbing, and nodded.

Uncle Jonah ran back to the Buick. The driver’s door had been smashed and at first try would not budge. Hot metal and burning oil filled his nose. Billowing flames lapped out from under the car and smoke crept from under the hood. He stared at the pinned woman in the doomed car, his mind racing towards solutions. She stared back, screaming she didn’t want to die.

Placing his hands, claw-like, under the edges of the door and bracing a foot on the side of the car, Uncle Jonah pulled. The woman continued screaming for her life. Uncle Jonah joined her with his own screams of pain. Metal screamed on metal.

He fell backwards as the door came open at the insistence of his brute force.

Picking himself up off the ground, he was once again at her side. The flesh of his hands singed and hot, so hot he stopped feeling the pain there, nerve-ending overload. Black smoke enveloped them. He grabbed the steering wheel and pushed hard. With a plastic pop, the whole steering column moved, but only a quarter inch. He jumped, afraid he might have hurt the woman, but he hadn’t. The wheel had moved and it was enough to slide the woman out from beneath it.

Gently, gently Uncle Jonah lifted the broken and bruised and bloody woman and soon was planting her by her daughter's side in bedewed grass going dry through fiery heat evaporation. The pines seemed to grow taller as shadows danced on the ground around their trunks.

The old Buick creaked with heat on the highway before exploding, rocking in on itself, sending metal meteors flying through the night.

"Stay here and wait for help," Uncle Jonah told the mother and daughter. He then ran to his truck to call for help.

She was being loaded onto a stretcher board, her neck braced, by EMTs when the state trooper arrived.

"What happened, ma'am?" the trooper asked.

"I came 'round the corner just as the semi was coming the other way. I think the blue car crossed the line and ran right into the semi. None of us had time to stop."

"You got out of your car by yourself?" the trooper asked.

"No. Someone else helped us out. Some man. He saved me and my daughter."

"You're lucky. The cars have all blown, looks like."

The EMTs loaded her into an ambulance, her daughter, still sobbing, sitting at her side.

"Who was it, ma'am?" the trooper asked.

"I dunno."

The rear doors closed. The ambulance sped away, sirens screaming around trees.

A fire crew was having a tough time fighting the fires. Flames danced yellow-orange, sometimes with a hint of blue or green.

"Sir?" a firefighter approached the trooper. "We got another body over here."

Standing at the side of the semi's cab, door open, the trooper stared in at the motionless body of Uncle Jonah. Dear Uncle Jonah sat in his cab, a massive and open head wound leaking vital fluids.

"I wonder if this is the man that helped that mother and daughter," the trooper postulated.

The firefighter shook his head. "I doubt it. EMTs said, considering that wound, he likely hit his head on the steering wheel and died on impact."

FUN WITH LATEX, PAINT AND OATMEAL

BY TRACY NELSON

I just wanted to mess around with doing some FX one night, and here is what I ended up with.

I laid down a coat of liquid latex on my arm and let it dry to a tacky consistency.

Then I dropped some oatmeal on it for texture and carefully tamped it down. I let that dry. Then I did another coat of liquid latex over that.

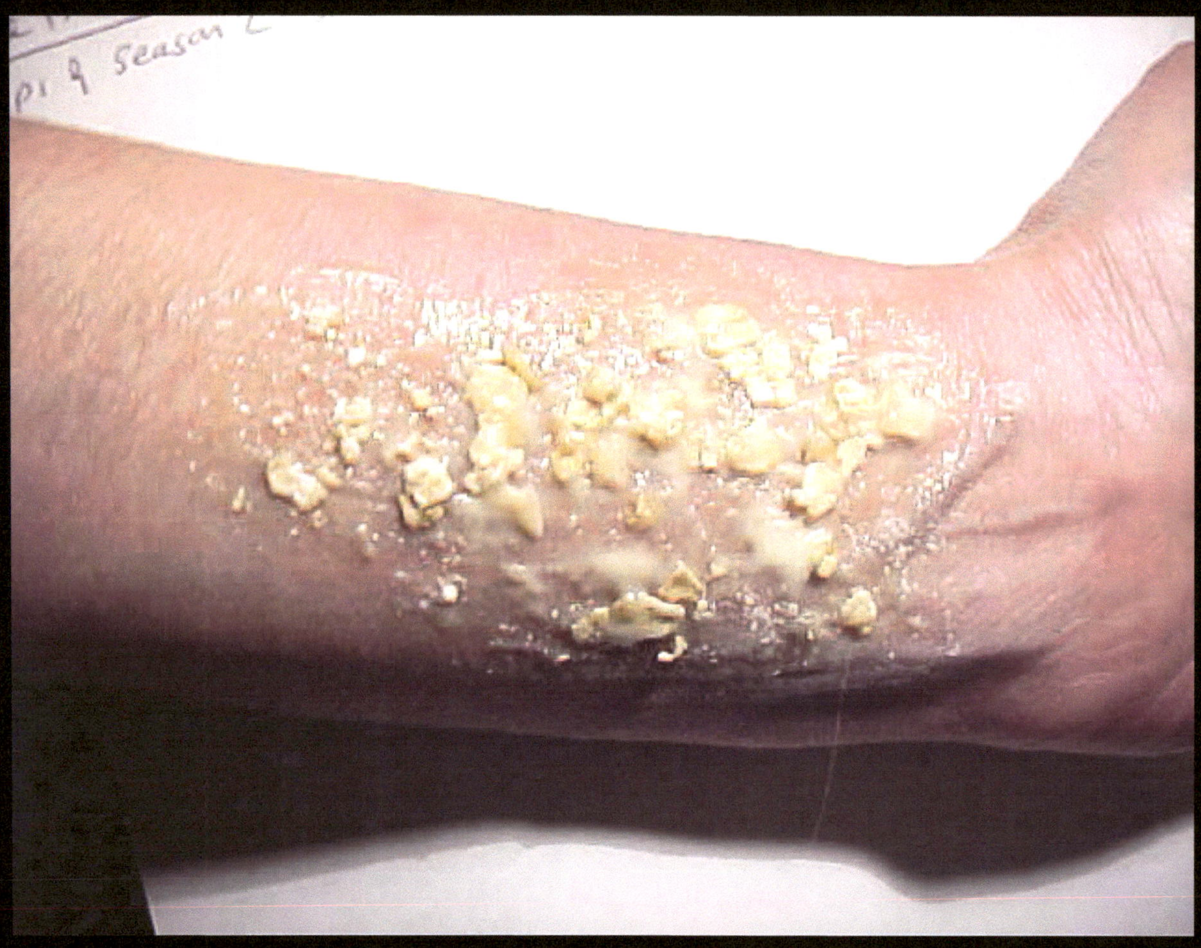

Once dried, I played with paint.

I started with black to make seams/outlines and a little green and yellow here and there to make it look infected. But it was the black paint mixed with bright red that really made it look GROSS (the money shot).

I had a lot of fun with it and I can only say that the pics don't show how really cool this quick effect looks, especially from different angles and lightings.

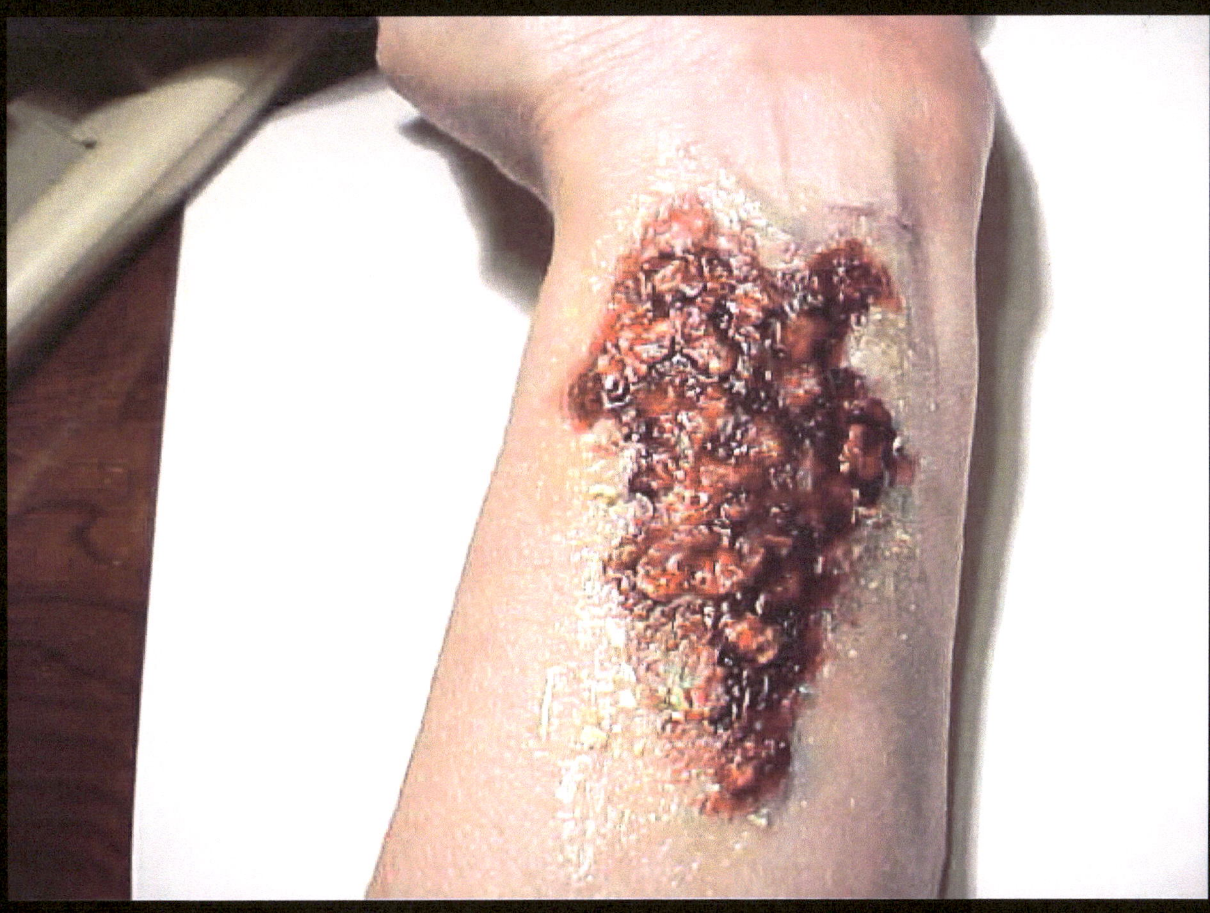

This was fun to play with and test out!

I first noticed Kurtis Primm's work on the wonderful HauntForum boards and was immediately impressed. He was obviously a kindred spirit, as he is to virtually ANY horror/Halloween enthusiast. We featured his yard haunt along with some of his excellent prose in HM #2, and we have gotten A LOT of feedback about his awesome "Peanuts/Great Pumpkin" yard display (check his other cool stuff at primmsylvania.webs.com).

*Kurtis sent us this absolutely masterful work of Halloween poetry for this issue, and I just gotta say...*The Harvest Moon *is one of the very best poems I have ever read so far about our favorite holiday. Kurtis captures the imagery, spirit and overall feeling of the season. You can almost smell the leaves and feel the autumn brushed winds as you read his stirring words.*

THE HARVEST MOON – Kurtis Primm

The harvest moon shines overhead
Above the fields of walking dead
The world is bathed in silvery beams
The harvest moon of Halloween

Casting shadows on the walls
Of werewolves and their howling calls
The silver moon light on the streets
To light the way for Tricks Or Treats

Oh, harvest moon of Halloween
Illuminate this spooky scene
An ever watchful eye so bright
See all there is to see tonight

Your moon beams shine
on hidden gnolls

To light the doors of
goblin holes

The fairy folk all dance
and sing

Beneath your shining silver beams

You shine upon the haunted house

Where spirits dwell and move about

A spotlight as the zombies rise

A twinkle in the black cats eyes

The harvest moon there shining bright

Adds magic to this spooky night

So sing your scary haunting tune

And dance beneath the harvest moon

Witches up and kick their heels

While stirring pots of monster meals

You shine upon the corn in rows

While bathing scarecrows on their poles

You shine upon the pumpkins skin

A light outside, alight within

The bats at night all swoop and swoon

A silhouette against the harvest moon

NEXT ISSUE: OCTOBER!! MORE PAGES!!

Halloween Machine looks at the different ways that Halloweenies celebrate their favorite month of the year!

Plus: Halloween Store Sightings, Kurtis Primm, and more of the haunted Halloween hoots and howls you've come to expect!

P.S. GO SEE "PARANORMAN!"

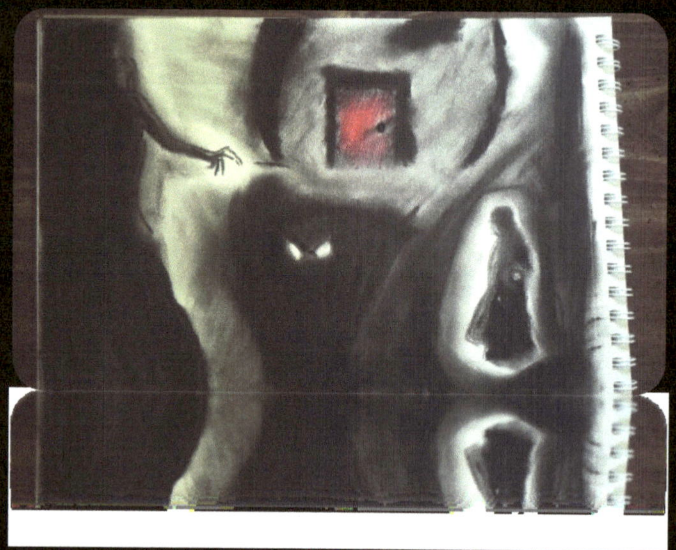

If you'd like to see your own stuff in the pages of

HALLOWEEN MACHINE

Please send poems, artwork, how-tos, haunt pictures, anything Halloween related to: unclesteed@hotmail.com

Above drawing: JESSE RAY COUNELIS / Back cover drawing: DIAMOND COUNELIS

www.ingramcontent.com/pod-product-compliance
Ingram Content Group UK Ltd.
Pitfield, Milton Keynes, MK11 3LW, UK
UKHW060122300726
14090UKWH00002B/310
9781300151432